HYLTON CAMPANOZZI BORROR

SWITCHED™

Created by
DEVIN HYLTON

Written by
DEVIN HYLTON & CHRIS CAMPANOZZI

Art by
MONTY BORROR

Lettered by
FRANZISCA GUEDEL & DARYL GILLHAM

For Markosia Enterprises Ltd

HARRY MARKOS
Publisher & Managing Partner

IAN SHARMAN ■ GM JORDAN ■ ANDY BRIGGS
Group Editors

AAM/MARKOSIA

Published by Markosia Enterprises, PO BOX 3477, Barnet, Hertfordshire, EN5 9HN. FIRST PRINTING, February2013. Harry Markos, Director.

ISBN: 978-1-905692-89-7

CHAPTER ONE

Present day New York on the planet Earth in the Milky Way Galaxy.
ROLLING HEIGHTS GENE
Look at me, Michael. Over here, smile for daddy.
Sally, honey. It's your daddy. Look at you, so beautiful.
SKYLLEU TOOSLEA BOOTHS NOTINED SIE QUILL.
WHYLLETRS NOOLDEES NOOTHSLOOKING DOONSERRS SIE EARTH. TROLLEYS BNNOLLDGES SIMON. *
*Translation: Lords of Quill world. Please look after our only hope. My newborn son of Earth named Simon.

SJ DAVID
SWITCHED

It's amazing to see them like this isn't it?
AH... SYNOTS..TE..
I'm sorry? Do you speak English?
Ah..Yes.. Yes I do.
Sorry. It is not my-how do you say-native language.
That's okay.
If you don't mind my asking.
How is it that you are up and around so fast? Are you not the boy's mother?
Ah...Yes.. I mean no.
I am the boys...guardian, you would call it here.
I..I'm sorry.
This is none of my business. My adrenaline is going, you know?
To see my little boy.
Maybe one day our kids will play together, huh?
That would be nice.

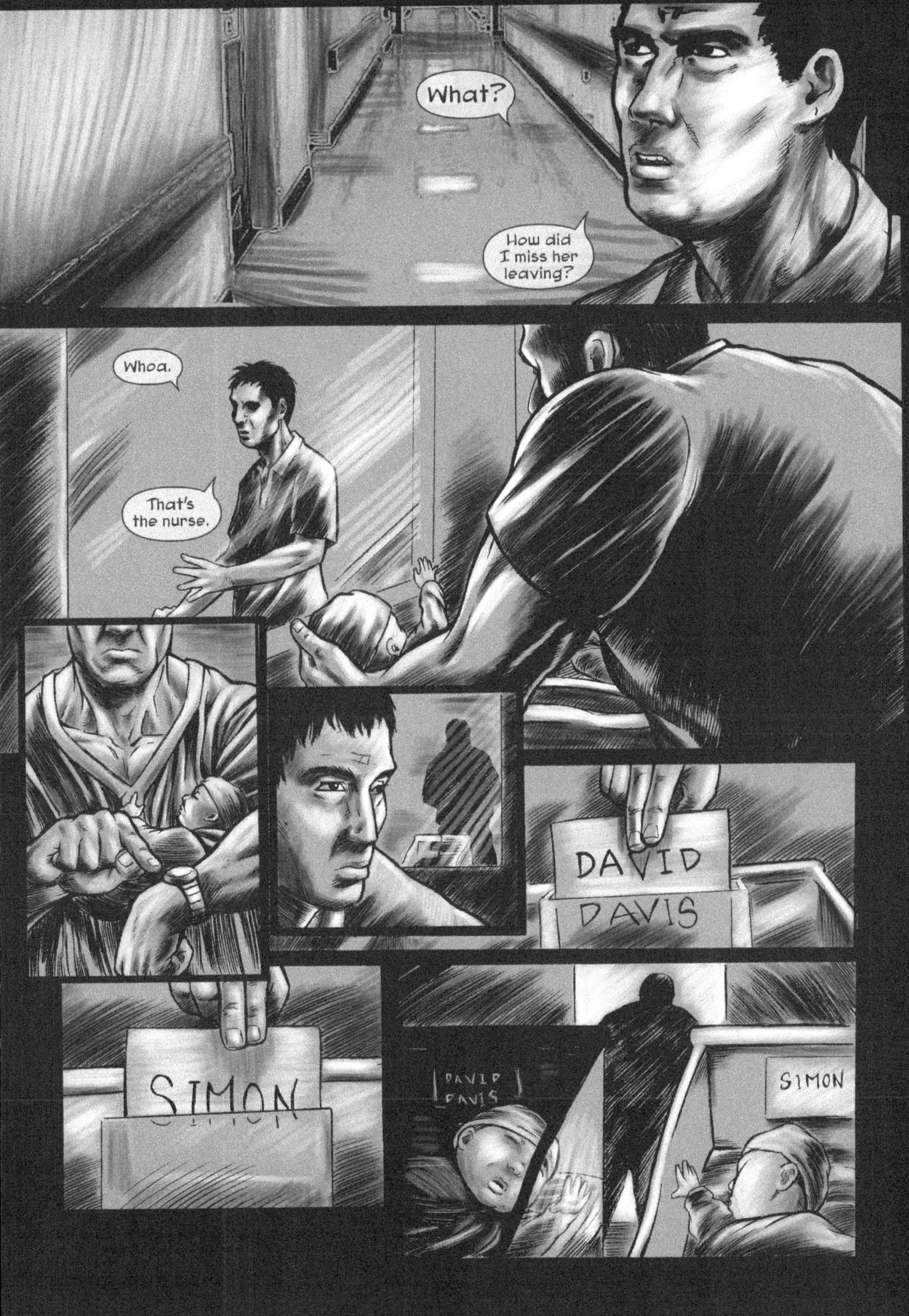
What?
How did I miss her leaving?
Whoa.
That's the nurse.
DAVID DAVIS
SIMON
DAVID DAVIS
SIMON

Who wants to see their new born son?
Here is your son. David Davis.
I'm so proud of you honey.
Hello. Sweetheart, I'm your mommy.
THUMP
THUMP
What are these?
I...I have no idea.

Ah, Miss Victoria. Here is Simon. He seems fine our doctors assure us.
He is very healthy and all vitals are good.
SYLLES NOTCTRINA URILLS*.
*Translation: All is lost, they know.
Now.
We have a child welfare worker downstairs that would like to ask you some questions.
This is standard procedure when.........
Arrgh!
You may leave now Miss Victoria.
I'll handle your release.

Two hours later.
I am so sorry child of Earth. You are not ready for what you will have to endure.
WHOOSH!
I will help you little one. As much as I can. But you will have to be strong.
Our world will depend on your bravery and leadership.
SWOOSH!
I have left your "brother" here on earth clues to find us my adopted son.
Hopefully his Stones of Peril and the kindness of the human species will be enough for him to survive here.
AHILLA SIE TOOSELEA HILAS DF BNNOLLDEGES. *
SWOOSH!
*Translation: May the lords keep you my son.

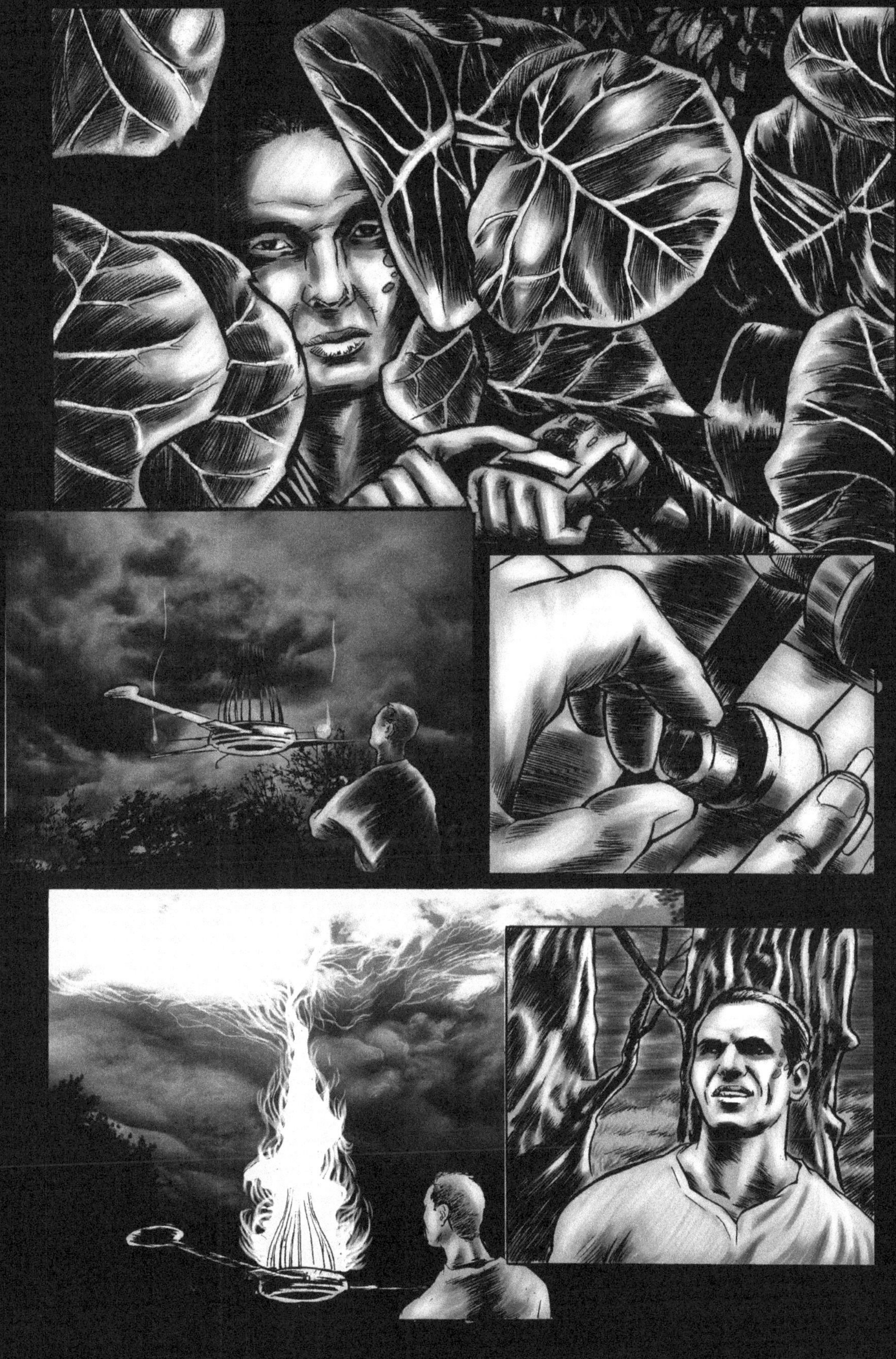

Rolling Heights NY. Home of mister and misses Davis and their son David. Twelve years later.

The Zellen boundaries of the Quill world. Home to dethroned princess Victora and her son Simon. Twelve earth years later.

Simon! What are you doing! You would have been destroyed by now.
BLAM!
SWOOSH!
BLAM!
BLAM!
Arrgh!

Simon.
It is only one GARNED *, till your trials.
You know what will happen to you, if you perform poorly.
*Translation: month.
Mother.
I am doing all that I can.
Most children at the academy know I am different then them.
No!
You are not different! You are my son and I....
I love you so much...
Human or not, You're my son and I raised you and...
You most grow into the warrior that our people need you to be!
Please mother, do not cry.
I will do my best to restore your name to the thrown of the Quill world.
Your son will defend us from the Sleegoth and Dar Khan.
Even if it kills me.

Hey!
WOOMP.
Hey David.
Ladies, ladies ladies.
Do..Ah.. Do you have a date for the eight grade dance yet?
He... He...He.
Do I have a date?
Well, let's see...
I have about five dates, so where do you think you'd fit in?
I..Ah, I'm sorry I asked.
Would David Davis report to the principals office please.
Saved By the bell ladies.
Let's meet back here tomorrow, however.
See if David's little black book can make some room.

David please come in.
Your parents and I where discussing your latest, "outburst."
First off. It's not my fault I know more about science than Mr. Pepper.
That fool, wouldn't know a frog's spleen from it's liver.
Be that as it may, David.
Calling your teacher a, what was it?
Jackanape
Ah yes, well...that was..ah.
No need to pretend that you know what it means, sir.
Out side right now young man.
We'll deal with you in a minute.

As you can see, David acts out a lot, he is becoming a problem.
SLAM
You think this is a problem, try living with him.
Frank!
There are many schools that might be more suited to David's "abilities."
Are they taking new kids now, because I have cash.
All right. That's it!
The minute a child is different. Everyone can't wait to label them as a "problem" or "different."
You two need to realize that our our child will grow up to be a scientist or a doctor and probably change the world.
Good day principal Simmons. You and my husband both need to learn how to deal with my David. He's not some alien you know! He's a little man who could use guidance from both of you!
Get up Frank, I'll deal with you when we get home.
SLAM
Miss Collins.
Yes sir?
Do you know what Jackanape means?

Tell me spy.
How is the "earth" boy handling his training.
As to be expected your excellency.
The boy is slow in mind and body. His mother tries but no matter what she passes on to him, it will not be enough.
It was for told that in this millennium, the Quill's queen would birth a son who could defeat me.
That one day, our race would fall to the Quill.
To bad the elders could not foresee my brilliance.
I want you to make sure that this boy fails at everything, you understand?
No matter how "gifted" her real son is, he will never find his way here from Earth.
Yes, Dar Khan. Your name shall ring for ever more on this planet.
See that it does.

Well, we where hoping you could help the boy.
Odds are, he's just board with regular junior high work.
Well, I don't see why not, I've dealt with a lot of intelligent high strung children.
If you don't mind my asking.
You are a highly respected psychologist.
What are you doing working with "special" children in the suburbs of New York?
You could have your own television show, for crying out loud.
Well, children are our future, correct?
Honestly, there have been several physical and intellectually exceptional children born in this town.
Call it professional curiosity.
Yes, we are a proud little berg, maybe there is something in the water?
Speaking of which. Would you care for a coffee?
Yes, extra milk if you have it.
Closer and closer.
ROLLING HILLS YOUTH BREAKS TRACK AND FIELD RECORDS

Math class.
a2=b2+c2, Next!
English class.
"April is the curliest month." Opening line to TS Elliot's "The Waste land."
Why are we still dealing with nouns and verbs, when we could be dissecting what passes for poetry?
Art class.
Is this what you mean when you say "Draw your favorite park?"
Music class.
Clearly, I can play "hot cross buns" is it?
When are we getting to Mozart or Brahms?
Health class.
STD ?
You must be joking?!

Paratronics class.
HEKLYH NOTTELDBED CLOSSDER. *
*Translation: Please I am lost. Explain again.
Weapons training.
Blast one, unlock than load. Firing three blasts per minute.
No! Again!
Tactical training.
Four clicks north and seven meters to the west.
No! Again!
Battle of the lake goth!
(Trust us, you don't want to know.)
Roar!

Arrgh!
WHAMP!
Arggh!
Enough!
Auggh!
Roooar!
Hooray!
Hooray!
Hooray!

WOOMP
Auggh.
ROAR!
WOOMP
Arrgh!

Simon! Simon!
Down with the Sleegoth! Down with the Sleegoth!
Simon! Simon!
Down with the Sleegoth!
Simon! Simon!
Down with the Sleegoth!
Down with the Sleegoth! Down with the Sleegoth!
The boy is becoming a problem.
Did you see my lord? A traitor to you, helped him by throwing him a blaster weapon.
Then we will just need to crush their new found spirit. Double the size of our army. Ration the distribution of food.
I'll turn this boy into the most hated being in this galaxy.

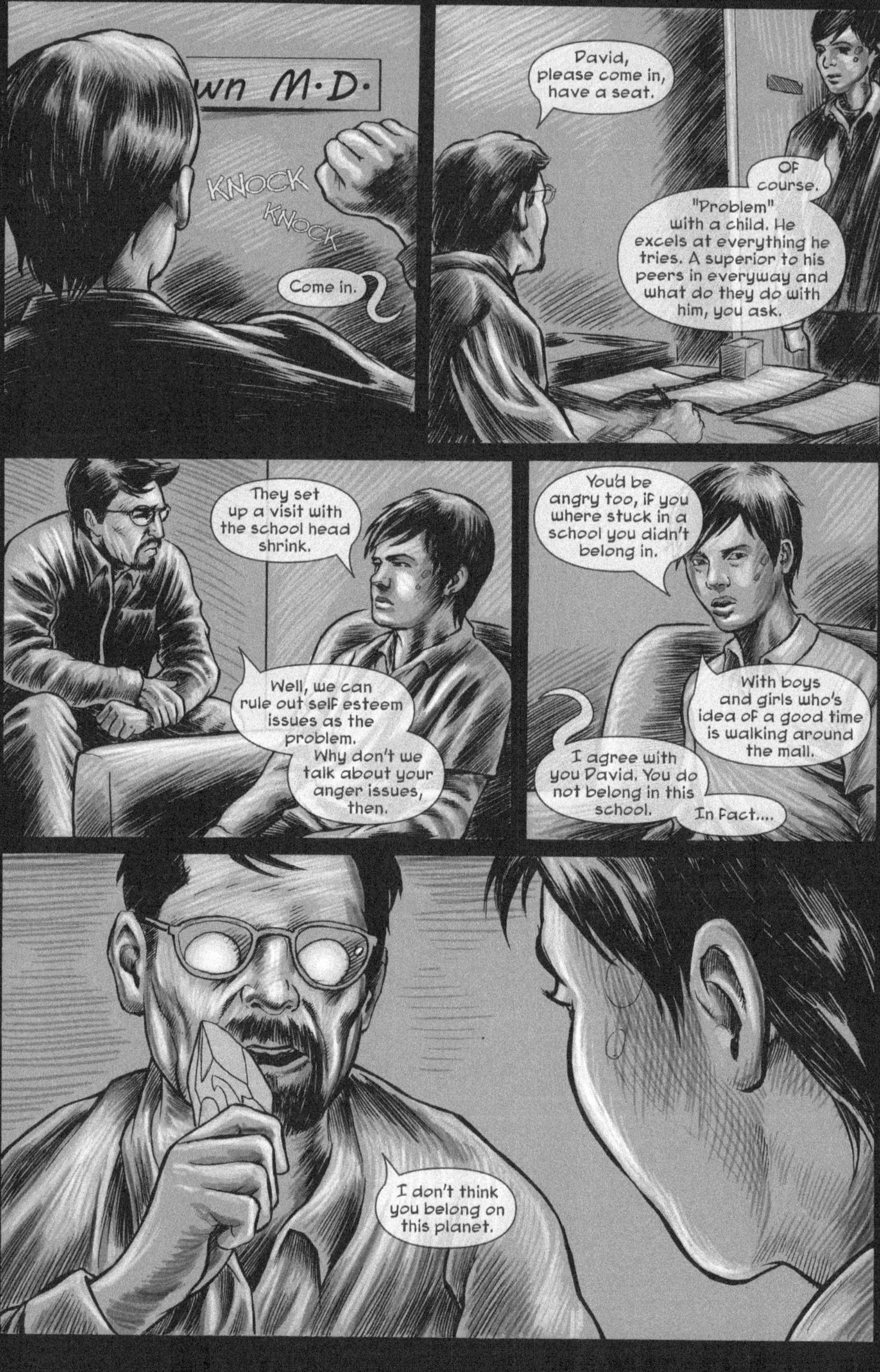
wn M·D·
KNOCK
KNOCK
Come in.
David, please come in, have a seat.
Of course.
"Problem" with a child. He excels at everything he tries. A superior to his peers in everyway and what do they do with him, you ask.
They set up a visit with the school head shrink.
Well, we can rule out self esteem issues as the problem.
Why don't we talk about your anger issues, then.
You'd be angry too, if you where stuck in a school you didn't belong in.
With boys and girls who's idea of a good time is walking around the mall.
I agree with you David. You do not belong in this school.
In fact....
I don't think you belong on this planet.

CHAPTER TWO

Mongrel members of the Quill race. You are now no longer allowed out of your dwellings past the setting of our solar sphere.
All able bodied Quill are to report to local military indoctrination centers.
Or in the words of your elders.
ARFFECT DETERC DAR KHAN!*
*Translation: All hail Dar Khan!

There these Quill are easy enough to manipulate. Few are warriors and if we keep them divided they will be unable to mount any resistance.
My lord. What of the boy Simon and his mother. They still may posses Stones of Peril.
What of the Quill boy on Earth, my lord?
If she left him any stones he could come back here. And.. well..
Even with Peril Stones an "earth" boy would not have the physical abilities to truly master them.
You may have a point. These Earth creatures are more "sophisticated" then I gave them credit for.
Translate a message to our Sleegoth warrior on Earth.
The Quill boy can not be permitted to survive.
Like the rocks you where born with?
How, how do you have a stone?
I've studied every earth geology paper I could find and I've never seen another one like....

I'm about to be very honest with you David.
I am a child psychologist for one reason and one reason only.
I've met others. Like you born with amazing physical and mental abilities.
All of them had these with them at the time of their birth.
David. What I am about to tell you may be hard to hear but.
I believe that you are a member of an alien race that has visited Earth on more than one occasion.
You..You mean I could visit my home planet?!
I've placed three of these stones together.
When I have. They begin to create what I theorized was a door way to your possible home world.
Possibly yes. I need to see the other stones David. May I see them?
Doctor; if what you are saying is true.
Then why was I brought here?
Or more importantly........
Why was I cast out of my world?

Where is he!
Then you will never say anything again.
I...I will never tell you.
No!
Let her go!
Or what little one, what can you do to me?
Fine. You win.
We'll go.

David. I've been meaning to ask you.
Why where you not more shocked when I brought up that you where not of this world?
I...I think I always knew.
All kids feel like they don't fit in.
However, in my case. There was no doubt.
The stones are the key.
They have been here before, all exceptional children. Almost like...
Yes, an experiment. They where experimenting to see if something would work.
Oh my lord! Look at the door!
Mom?! Dad?!
David, wait!

You.
Quill warrior, pray to what ever you where raised to worship.
Dar Khan wants you eliminated.
Not used to dealing with someone with your own enhanced strength.
This will be easy.
Why... What is happening?!
I'll explain it to you Mrs. Davis.
If we live that long.
Son! Watch out!
You underestimate me Neanderthal.
You don't know what "special" kids do on this world; do you?
They take Judo classes!
Arrgh!
CRASH

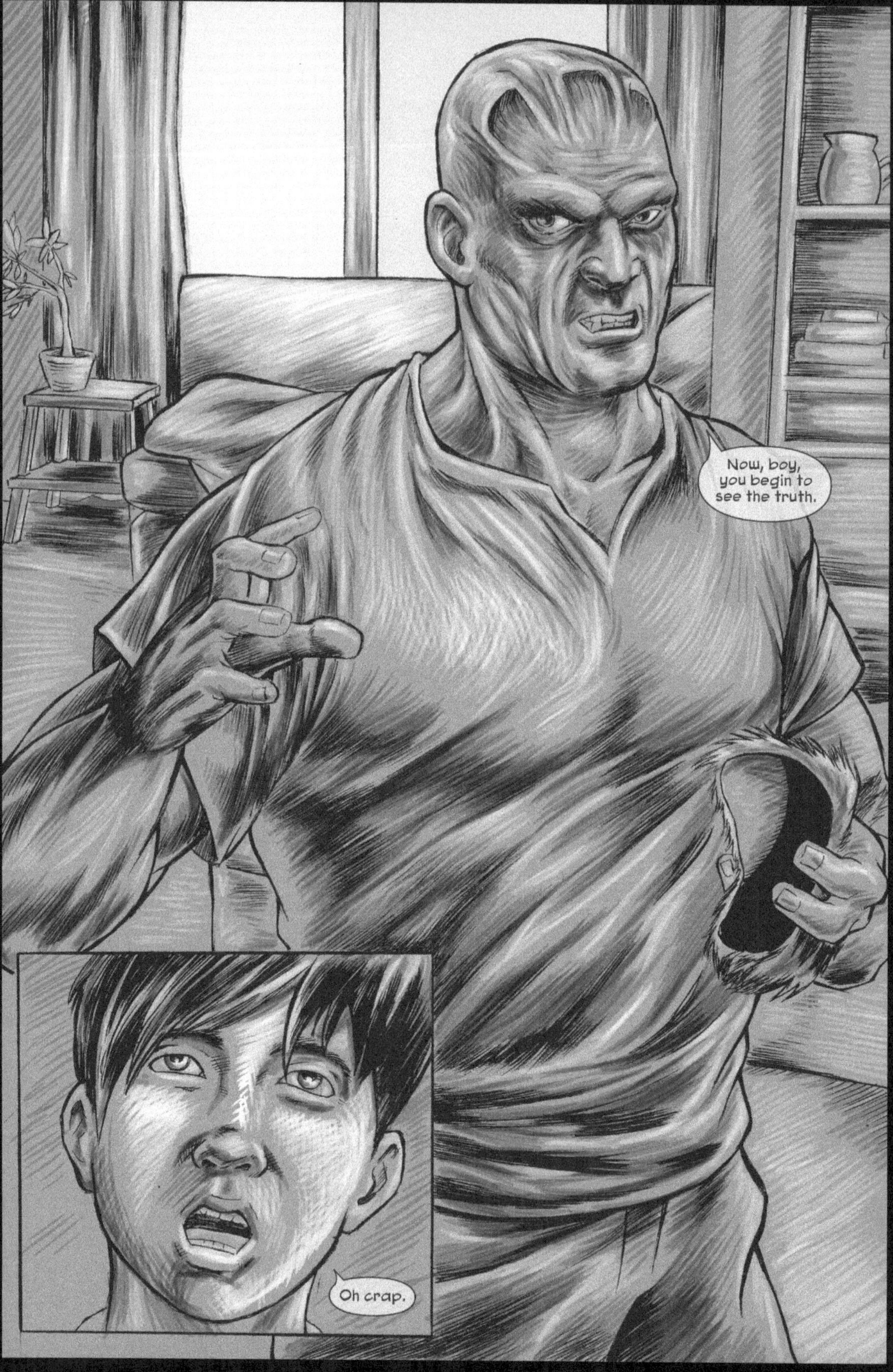
Now, boy, you begin to see the truth.
Oh crap.

Dr. Brown!
Third drawer on the left, the stones!
Got it!
Dar Khan entrusted me to finish you off and I will!
Let go of my son!
WHAM!
Auggh!
David!
Heads up!
A stone of Perilous! Of the PERIL!
No!

Please
Quill prince!
WOOM!
Spare
me!

Quill parasites, you are about to be joined by the one who only days before..
You where foolish enough o cheer his name.
Behold! Simon the prince of the Quill!
Your only hope, ha! Ha!
Fear not, Quill warrior.
I know that you are strong.
Don't mock me. I've suffered much today.
I would never mock one such as you.
I will die for you and what I believe you fight for.
Thank... Thank you.
It is important that we escape.
Few have ever escaped a Sleegoth prison and those who have...
May have wished they did not.
Please, my mother is here! I must save her!
No my champion.
You must save us all.

Mr. And
Mrs. Davis.
As hard as
this is to hear
and judging by
what you've just
witnessed.
I believe
that your son
David is...Well...
Mother,
Father.
I am from
another planet or
what I also theories
may be another
dimension.
I know this
is hard to hear,
however now with
Dr. Brown's help.
I may
be able to
return.
Return?!
Wha..
What do you
mean!?
Are you
leaving us?
I don't
know what
to say.
I have
to know who
I really am and
where I come
from.
Please
understand.
We do son.
We do.
Sooo....
How do you
get back to
your world?
Anyway.
Oh no.
POLICE
DIAL 911
POLICE
We must
go, now!

Quickly, we need an open field and the stones!
Suspects are on the run. Need back up.
Back up is on the way.
Go! I'll handle this!
Frank! No!
Dad!
On the ground now! Hands on your heard!
Arrgh!
You have the right to remain silent....
Give em hell son.

Quickly, place the stones in a circle pattern.
This will open a door way?
That is my theory, yes.
That should be it.
David. It's up to you now.
VOOM!
Wait a minute, here!
If you think I'm letting my boy go in there alone.
You are mistaken doctor.
Mrs. Davis you can't possible think...
Fine, then we all go!
There is no time for this. I may need all your help in that world.
Freeze. Hands on your heads!
Now!
Arrgh!

WOOSH!
You three!
Is everyone okay?
I wonder if we are alive or dead.
My lord.
What be this? Two Quill spies?!
I think not. Their ridicules robes give them away.
To the detention center with you three.
We may have not thought this plan threw all the way.

CHAPTER THREE
BORROR

So it was you who tossed me that blaster weapon.
Is that why you are in here?
Yes, that and speaking out against the Sleegoth.
I know of the teachings. That the son of queen Victor will defeat the Sleegoth once and for all.
I will do what ever is necessary to help you my prince.
Dump them with the Quill prince and his supporter.
This way they will see what happens when you defy Dar Khan!
Well I think it is clear that I was sent to Earth to be spared this.
Yes, this Dar Khan seems to be a tyrant on this world like the ones on our own.
You. I... I know you.
Stranger. There is something about you. That I cannot....
You. You are... Oh my God!
You two look...a like, don't you?
We... We were switched.
I was sent to Earth and you... You took my place... Here.

This must have been the work of Dar Khan. That is why you...What are you called?
David. David Davis.
You are our champion. It is your job to save the Quill world.
How could I do that?
I know nothing of this world. This Dr. Khan, would have all the advantage.
But I do.
I know everything about this world, our weaponry, our enemy.
Together we could stop the Sleegoth.
I don't know. How or why should we even trust you?
Because....
He is my son.
Your whole life we knew you were different.
David.
We knew you didn't fit in.
This, this is what you where meant to do.
Help them, help their people be free.
Of course, mother.
But what can we do from here?
I believe I can help you my prince.

I have studied the ways of the ancient Quill. They where a people of great inner peace and spirit.
They also studied sorcery. I know a way to combine what both of you know.
You will be one in the same and yet different.
My mother is in danger; I will do what ever I have to do to free her and our people.
I concur. This Dar Khan, his type never stops. If he knows of Earth. He will try to dominate my world as well.
We must all join hands to make this work. Quickly; before the guards return.
WEEKMNE YOTHELL ROOMDS DO.
NOORMATNED NERDFGOOL FROSSDELLS.
RELLSA RESTURMS NOORDSFT COORKIDNTS.*
*Translation: These brothers separated by worlds now rejoined. One of body and mind, they will be forever more.
Arrgh!
Arrgh!
No! She's killing them!
Wait, wait! Look... Look at that!

Now, now my teachings make sense to me.
It's like my mind is open for the first time.
My self as well. I...I all the knowledge you accumulated here.
This, this is how I was mean to feel and think.
Amazing.

What! What is the meaning of all this!
Auggh!
All of you. Stay here and stay safe take this blaster for protection.
There is one thing I need you to do for me my beautiful sorceress.
You know my mother. Please free her and bring her back here, to wait with you all in safety.
Of course, my prince.
The only way that the two of us can bring down Dar Khan is to fight him one on one, we won't be able to muster any type of army this quickly.
I agree.
The Quill planet and Earth have several things in common Dictators and...
Mass media.

Two hours later.
My name is Simon Victor. I amt he Quill prince, son of queen Victor!
This is my brother from the planet Earth named David, son of the Davis!
We challenge the mighty Dar Khan for the rule of the Quill world.
Ready my weapons.
I have a prince to dethrone.
The winner rules. The loser leaves the planet never to return.

Was it wise to infuriate Dar Khan like that?
This battle will be hard enough as is.
We need him here and we need him angry.
Anger leads to many mistakes.
Children!
So two princes will die today instead of one.
I agree with broadcasting this to the planet.
Less talking more blasting!
WOOMP!
Nothing will assure my God hood on this planet than destroying the likes of you two.
BLAM!
I hope you didn't think this would end that easily!
I destroyed many a Sleegoth warrior to rise to power.
Remember our warrior training!
We need to fight together!
You two will be even easier.

Uggh!
Look out!
WOOM!
WHAMP!
Arrgh!
Arrgh!
SWOOSH!
WOOM!
No!
Arrgh!
You're next, boy prince.
COME AND FACE ME!

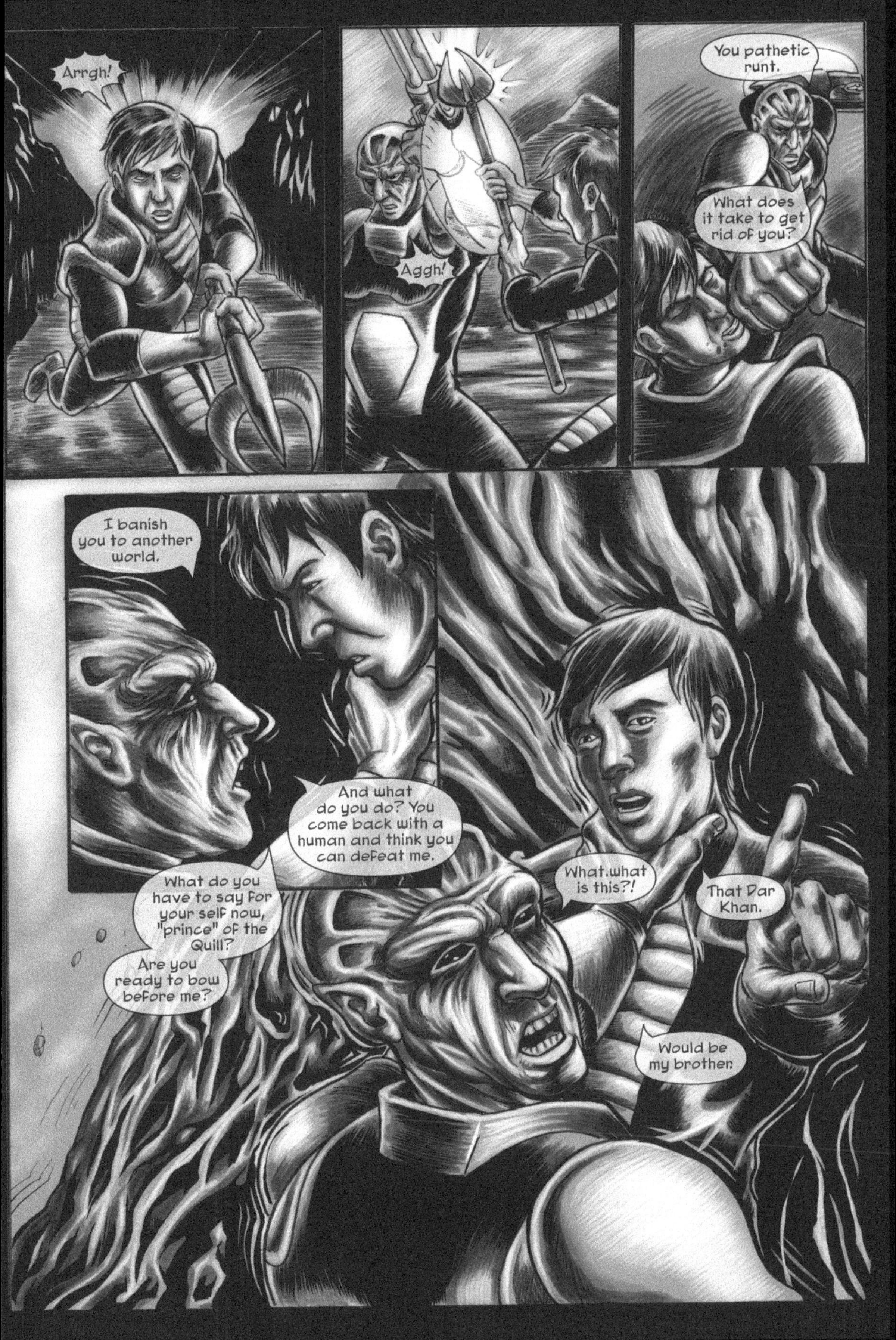
Arrgh!
Aggh!
You pathetic runt.
What does it take to get rid of you?
I banish you to another world.
And what do you do? You come back with a human and think you can defeat me.
What do you have to say for your self now, "prince" of the Quill?
Are you ready to bow before me?
What.what is this?!
That Dar Khan.
Would be my brother.

Riding a very large Lake Goth!
Nooo!
What made you think to get a Lake Goth?
Not really fair is it?
Chalk it up to my "human" side.

My people, Dar Khan is no more!
The day of the Quill has returned!
Hooray!
Hooray!
Hooray!
Hooray!
Sleegoth! You have one day to retreat from this world or you will be held accountable for your actions.
That's my boy.

Two days latter.
I am a Peril "stones" throw away if you ever need my help again.
My brother. I cannot thank you for all that you have done.
Thanks to you. The Quill will prosper once again.
When you return home.
Remember to find and keep all the Peril stones.
They could be quite dangerous in the wrong hands.
Thank you for raising my boy.
Thank you for doing the same.
Now that I know the mystery of the stones, what shall I do with my life's work ?
You could always right a fictional piece about all this. It would make a great comic book.
I'm just glad you are coming home with us dear. I was afraid you might want to stay.
Are you kidding... Earth is my home Besides...
Some one has to break dad out of jail.

What now my son?
Now we bring the Quill world into a new age, of hope and prosperity.
That will be hard for one man to accomplish on his own.
I know. The family Victor will need to grow and grow.
What? my prince.. I...
Now.
With my own queen at my side. Nothing can stop me.
Children. Children beat me.
An Earth child at that!
Maybe we should have sent him to a different planet?
I hear there is little life on Mars.

The Quill world, twenty years later.
My lord! My lord!
Lord Victor. We've just picked up a trans mission from space.
A Sleegoth armada is headed for our atmosphere.
Set all army captains on their highest alert.
Father. I am ready you have taught me well. I will not let our family name down.
My son, I hoped you would never have to fight the Sleegoth.
I know my son.
However, I think I will need even more family to help in this battle.
I just hope that my brother is in a position to send aid from Earth.

Earth, also twenty years later.
ELECTION RESULTS
NILBOG
Governor Davis will soon be sworn in as our forty fifth president.
For the first time in history a third party independent candidate carried so many states in the union. Governor Davis created his own Intergalactic Party.
During his time as a Navy Seal Governor Davis rescued several shipping captains from Somali pirates.
9News:Election Results| Breaking News
Vote Talley LANDSLIDE
Now we begin a new chapter in US history.

I Simon Davis do solemnly swear that I will faithfully execute the office of President of the United Sates.
And will to the best of my ability preserve, protect and defend the constitution of the United Sates.
My fellow Americas. Today I pledges to do all I can to defend this nation.
We have many enemies here at home and abroad. In the past this country has aided other in need. That is part of our history and part of our character.
This will not change under my watch.
I...I have seem much in my life. I've seen evil and I've seen what happens when that evil is allowed to spread.
We have always argued in this country about using our might. However, no one can argue that when good people do nothing evil triumphs.
Freedom is the right of all men and women on this shore and those shores that some would argue are not ours to interfere with.

SCHOOOM!
SCHOOOM!
SCHOOOM!

Under my watch, democracy will spread and I vow to aid anyone who needs our help.
No matter where the may be.

I call upon all Americans to fight with me for freedom,
liberty and hope for all life, everywhere.

SWITCHED CONCEPT ART

If the Sleegoth aliens seem familiar to some readers, then good. They damn well should. They are essentially based on the aliens we know so well and love from the late 70's and early 80's Japanese cartoons that managed to come to the US in my childhood. Yep, there is some Voltron there, and some Battle of the Planets (the US name) and a little bit of my own influence as well.

I based them off of the painting, seen here I did about 8 years ago, with the above influences in mind. In turn, I adjusted the original painting for the cover of the book as I was excited for this piece to finally have a home. If one is lucky, as an artist, things come full circle.

If you are of the sort, there are a few Easter Eggs in the art work you may find interesting... I'm not going to tell you what they are, of course. But that's all the fun. And once this turns into a job, and loses all the fun, that's when I quit. I'm sure you understand.

Montgomery Borror

San Francisco

2012

www.ingramcontent.com/pod-product-compliance
Ingram Content Group UK Ltd.
Pitfield, Milton Keynes, MK11 3LW, UK
UKHW061952290726
14090UKWH00021B/1200